Kathleen Bullock

A SURPRISE FOR MITZI MOUSE

5/02 JJ

SIMON AND SCHUSTER BOOKS FOR YOUNG READERS

Published by Simon & Schuster Inc., New York

SIMON AND SCHUSTER
BOOKS FOR YOUNG READERS
Simon & Schuster Building
Rockefeller Center
1230 Avenue of the Americas
New York, New York 10020

10 9 8 7 6 5 4 3 2 1
Library of Congress Cataloging–in–Publication Data
Bullock, Kathleen, 1946-
A surprise for Mitzi Mouse.
SUMMARY: Mitzi, a young mouse, resents the presence
of her new sister Fifi until she comes to like having
her around.
[1. Babies—Fiction. 2. Sisters—Fiction. 3. Mice—
Fiction] I. Title.
PZ7.B9144Su 1989 [E] 88-32778
ISBN 0-671-67331-9

To my sisters

—K.B.

At first, only Mitzi lived with her mommy
and daddy. And that's just the way she liked it.

All the toys belonged to Mitzi, and all the books.
In fact, everything in her cozy bedroom belonged
to her alone.

Mitzi was the apple of everyone's eye.

*Isn't Mitzi precious! So cute and so smart!
Sweet Mousiekins, our darling!*

Smile everybody.

Both her grandmothers,
and both her grandfathers,
and all her aunts and uncles
thought Mitzi was the
cutest little mouse alive.

But best of all, Mommy and Daddy always had time to play with her.

They never said, "Go away, Mitzi, I'm busy now."
or "Hush, Mitzi, don't be so noisy."

A is for Alligator.
B is for Bear.

My mommy!

Back then, Mitzi could climb into her mother's lap
whenever she liked, and they would read together
from The Big ABC Book.

But that was before Fifi came to live with them. Mitzi didn't know where she came from, or why Mommy and Daddy thought she was so great.

They said: "We have a wonderful surprise for you, Mitzi—a darling little sister who will be your new friend."

Mitzi didn't like the sound of that.

"When is she leaving?"

Fifi looked like a tiny pink peanut with ears
and no hair! She couldn't walk, and she couldn't talk,
and she couldn't play. All she could do was lie
in her cradle and go "Goo Goo" all day.

"What's so special about that?" thought Mitzi. "I can stand on my head!" But Mommy and Daddy didn't notice her new trick. They were too busy looking at the peanut.

When Mitzi got tired of listening to everyone fuss over Fifi, she would go to her bedroom and sit on the floor with all of her toys around her. Sometimes she felt sad when she thought about Mommy's and Daddy's surprise.

One morning, Daddy set up a crib
for Fifi in Mitzi's room.

"Baby Fifi is too big now to sleep in a cradle
in our room. You and she will have a lot of fun
sharing a room together," said Daddy.

As soon as Daddy left, Mitzi jumped up and down in a fit. "I don't want to share my room with the peanut," yelled Mitzi. "No way! No way!"

Mitzi was in a bad mood all day. She grabbed her favorite book and marched up to her mother. "Read to me, please, Mommy?"

Mitzi's mother gave her a kiss and said, "Of course I'll read to my Mitzi. It's one of my favorite things to do."

Read to me, please!

Mitzi settled down just like old times. They read all the way up to "K is for Kangaroo" when a yowling came from the bedroom.

Mommy set Mitzi down. "I'm sorry, Honey. It's past baby's feeding time. We'll have to finish the book later."

"That baby is always butting in," pouted Mitzi.

"I don't think they love me at all anymore!"

Mitzi was so mad she took
her crayons and scribbled on the
kitchen wall. It wasn't even a
good picture. It was so ugly
you could tell she was mad.

Mommy and Daddy were angry at Mitzi. Daddy put her crayons away in a high cupboard until she learned to behave herself.

Mitzi had a little cry over that. Coloring was one of her favorite things to do.

Fifi was growing bigger every day. She crawled along the floor and played with Mitzi's toys.

Mitzi didn't like that,
and grabbed them away.

Fifi cried.

Mother said: "Let Fifi play with some of your toys, Mitzi. You have lots of toys, and it's good to learn how to share."

"No!" said Mitzi, stamping her foot. "Let her get her own toys!"

Mommy and Daddy went to the store and bought Fifi some toys. Mitzi was not happy. She looked at her own scruffy old toys—and then at Fifi's brand new ones.

She wondered if Fifi knew how to share.

Maybe Mitzi would share something with Fifi first. "I'll let you play with my rubber Ducky if you'll let me play with your new ball," she offered.

"Goo," said Fifi.

Mitzi thought that meant "sure" in Baby language, and they traded. Then Mitzi said, "Do you want to learn how to play ball?"

"Goo," said Fifi.

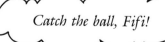

One day Mitzi noticed that Fifi knew how to walk.

She even said some words.

Mommy!
Fifi can walk!

Ball!
My ball!

Mommy thought Fifi was even big enough to enjoy
reading with them. She put Fifi on one knee and
Mitzi on the other, and started to read from
The Big ABC Book.

Fifi pointed at the pictures and giggled. Sometimes she drooled. That made Mitzi giggle, too.

Mitzi realized that sometimes she liked having Fifi around. "But she's still a peanut," she thought.

One day, Mitzi and Fifi were playing when Mommy and Daddy announced: "We have a wonderful surprise for you. Another darling baby is coming to live with us."

His name was Max, and he looked exactly like a pink peanut with no hair.

"Do you think you're going to like him?" asked Mitzi.

"No!" cried Fifi.

When is he leaving?

When Fifi toddled over to Mommy with
The Big ABC Book, Mommy was too busy
taking care of the new baby to read.

Daddy was too busy doing
everything else.

"I'll read to you, Fifi," said Mitzi. "I almost know
my ABC's now!"

And together they climbed into the rocking
chair and turned the pages of the book
and pretended that they knew how to read.

Sisters at last.